Dear Parent:
Your child's love of reading starts here!

Every child learns to read in a different way and at his or her own speed. Some go back and forth between reading levels and read favorite books again and again. Others read through each level in order. You can help your young reader improve and become more confident by encouraging his or her own interests and abilities. From books your child reads with you to the first books he or she reads alone, there are I Can Read Books for every stage of reading:

SHARED READING
Basic language, word repetition, and whimsical illustrations, ideal for sharing with your emergent reader

BEGINNING READING
Short sentences, familiar words, and simple concepts for children eager to read on their own

READING WITH HELP
Engaging stories, longer sentences, and language play for developing readers

READING ALONE
Complex plots, challenging vocabulary, and high-interest topics for the independent reader

ADVANCED READING
Short paragraphs, chapters, and exciting themes for the perfect bridge to chapter books

I Can Read Books have introduced children to the joy of reading since 1957. Featuring award-winning authors and illustrators and a fabulous cast of beloved characters, I Can Read Books set the standard for beginning readers.

A lifetime of discovery begins with the magical words **"I Can Read!"**

Visit www.icanread.com for information
on enriching your child's reading experience.

For Robby and Teddy
—J.O'C.

For Marie and Jack,
with love
—B.S.

I Can Read Book® is a trademark of HarperCollins Publishers.

Lulu and the Witch Baby. Text copyright © 1986, 2014 by Jane O'Connor. Illustrations copyright © 2014 by Bella Sinclair. All rights reserved. Manufactured in China. No part of this book may be used or reproduced in any manner whatsoever without written permission except in the case of brief quotations embodied in critical articles and reviews. For information address HarperCollins Children's Books, a division of HarperCollins Publishers, 10 East 53rd Street, New York NY 10022. www.icanread.com

Library of Congress Cataloging-in-Publication Data
O'Connor, Jane.
  Lulu and the witch baby / by Jane O'Connor ; illustrated by Bella Sinclair. — Revised and updated edition.
    pages cm — (I can read! Level 2)
  Originally published in a slightly different form in 1986.
  Summary: Lulu Witch begins to change her mind about her pesky baby sister when she thinks that one of her magic spells has made the baby disappear.
  ISBN 978-0-06-230517-6 (hardback) — ISBN 978-0-06-230516-9 (paperback)
  [1. Witches—Fiction. 2. Sisters—Fiction.] I. Sinclair, Bella, illustrator. II. Title.
PZ7.O222Lu 2014
[E]—dc23
                                                                                                              2013043185
                                                                                                              CIP
                                                                                                              AC

    14 15 16 17 18 SCP 10 9 8 7 6 5 4 3 2 1 ❖ Revised and updated edition, 2014

I Can Read!

READING 2 WITH HELP

Lulu *and the* Witch Baby

by Jane O'Connor
illustrated by Bella Sinclair

HARPER
An Imprint of HarperCollinsPublishers

Everybody loved Witch Baby.

Everybody but Lulu Witch.

She did not love Witch Baby at all.

Witch Baby got all the presents—
a bat rattle from Aunt Boo Boo,
a witch doll with a broomstick
from Cousin Hazel,
and a Dracula-in-the-box
from Uncle Fuzzy.

Nobody ever had time

for Lulu Witch anymore.

6

"Mama! Mama!" cried Lulu Witch.

"Watch me fly on my broom."

"Not now, dear," said Mama Witch.

"Papa! Papa!

Please fix my dollhouse," said Lulu Witch.

"Not now, dear," said Papa Witch.

Nobody ever got mad at Witch Baby.

Not even when she was bad.

And she was bad a lot.

Witch Baby was always
pulling Spot's tail.
Witch Baby was always
messing up Lulu's things.
One time, Witch Baby even spit food
at Lulu Witch.

"Witch Baby is just a baby,"

said Mama Witch.

"She thinks it is funny."

"Some joke," said Lulu Witch.

Lulu wished Witch Baby would
go away.

She wished Witch Baby
would go away forever.

Then one day Lulu got her wish.

It was a rainy day.

Lulu was drawing with her crayons.

"I must go to the market.

Will you watch Witch Baby?"
said Mama Witch.

"Yes, Mama," said Lulu Witch.

"I'll be back soon," said Mama Witch.

And away she flew.

Lulu went back to her drawing.

It was a drawing of a mother witch

and a little girl witch.

They were holding hands.

It was the best drawing
Lulu Witch had ever done.
She couldn't wait
to show it to Mama Witch.

Lulu was almost done

when she heard Spot barking.

She went to the back door

and let him in.

Then Lulu returned to finish her drawing.

Oh no! There was Witch Baby.

And there was the drawing.

In lots of little pieces!

17

Witch Baby smiled at Lulu

and said, "Goo-goo!"

She was not even sorry.

"Witch Baby, you are the worst baby ever," shouted Lulu Witch. "I wish you would disappear."

Then Lulu thought of the magic room

and the magic book of spells.

Mama Witch had told Lulu

never to go to the magic room.

But Lulu went anyway.

Lulu Witch found the magic book.

She turned the pages.

"Here is what I need," she said.

Slowly, Lulu read

the disappearing spell.

Disappearing Spell

Mix together

5 drops of bat blood

8 fly legs

1 cup of snake guts

2 cups of swamp water

17 hairs from a black cat

Lulu put everything in a big bowl.

"Drat!" she said.

"I need seventeen cat hairs.

There are only sixteen cat hairs

in the bottle."

Lulu hoped the spell

would work anyway.

Lulu stirred the magic stuff.

It turned brown and smelled funny.

Then she ran back to the living room.

Witch Baby was busy breaking

all of Lulu's crayons.

Lulu sprinkled the magic stuff

on Witch Baby's head.

"Good-bye, Witch Baby!" she shouted.

Lulu Witch closed her eyes
and counted to ten.

Then she opened her eyes.

Witch Baby was still there.

"Drat!" said Lulu Witch.

"The spell isn't working

because I didn't have enough cat hairs."

Back in the magic room,

Lulu washed the bowl.

She put away the magic book.

She had to clean up fast,

before Mama Witch got home.

Lulu hurried back to the living room.

Great goblins! Witch Baby was gone!

The spell had worked!

"Hooray!" shouted Lulu Witch.

"No more Witch Baby!"

Lulu Witch danced
around the room.

Then Lulu Witch thought
about Mama Witch.
Mama Witch was *not* going to be happy
that Witch Baby was gone.
Mama Witch was going to be mad.
Very, very mad!

Lulu Witch also thought

about Witch Baby.

Where *was* she?

Was Witch Baby all alone?

Was Witch Baby scared?

Lulu ran back to the magic room.

"I am a very wicked witch,"

she said, and she started to cry.

"I wish I had never made that spell.

I wish Witch Baby was back."

Lulu looked for a reappearing spell

in the magic book.

She could not find one.

So she made up some magic words
all on her own.
"Hocus pocus,
flip flapjack,
Witch Baby, Witch Baby,
please come back!"

Would her magic words work?

Lulu ran back to see.

38

There was Witch Baby!

"I did it!" cried Lulu Witch.

"I am a big girl witch.

I can make spells.

I can say magic words."

Witch Baby smiled at Lulu Witch
and said, "Goo-goo."
Lulu Witch gave Witch Baby a kiss.
"You are just a baby," she said.

"What a nice big sister!"

said Mama Witch.

"You are back!" cried Lulu Witch.

"Yes," said Mama Witch.

"When I came home,

Witch Baby was a mess.

There was sticky stuff all over her.

I took her into the bathroom

to wash her off."

"OH!" cried Lulu Witch.

The magic spell had not worked after all.

Deep down Lulu was glad.

"I was looking for you,"
Mama Witch told Lulu.
"Where were you?"

44

Lulu Witch looked down at her shoes.

"I was looking for Witch Baby,"
she said.

That was not really the truth.

But it was not really a lie.

"Look what I bought,"

said Mama Witch.

"A toadstool pie, your favorite."

Mama Witch and Lulu Witch
ate the toadstool pie.
They left a piece for Papa Witch.

Witch Baby had a bottle of brew.

She was too little to eat pie.

She was just a baby!